I DON'T WANT TO GO TO SCHOOL!

BY ALBERTO PELLAI
BARBARA TAMBORINI

ILLUSTRATED BY
ELISA PAGANELLI

EVERYONE SAYS KIDS NEED TO GO TO SCHOOL,
BUT IT'S BETTER TO STAY HOME.
I DON'T WANT TO GO!

EVERYONE SAYS THAT TEACHERS DON'T LET YOU TALK OR PLAY. THEY ARE MEAN. THEY ARE LOUD. AND THEY LET BATS FLY AROUND THE CLASSROOM!

BESIDES, THE WEATHER REPORT SAID IT MIGHT SNOW TODAY. HOW AM I SUPPOSED TO GET TO SCHOOL, THEN? ON A SLED?

EVERYONE KNOWS THAT IT'S ALWAYS COLD AT SCHOOL.
IT'S NOT WARM AND COZY LIKE AT HOME.

Oh, sweetheart, school is nothing like that.
It's warm and fun. The teachers are nice.
You'll get to play with friends and
do lots of things.

And... there will be a million things to do! You get to paint and draw with crayons and markers. You'll make friends to build forts and play tag with. The fun is endless.

OK, FINE. SCHOOL SOUNDS FUN.
BUT I WON'T SEE YOU ALL DAY.
I WILL MISS YOU WITH ALL MY HEART!

SO, WHY DON'T YOU COME TO SCHOOL WITH ME? JUST A FEW HOURS? WE
CAN DO ALL THE FUN THINGS THAT KIDS DO AT SCHOOL—PLAY, SING, DRAW.

DON'T YOU WANT TO STAY WITH ME, YOUR LITTLE CHICK?
AND THEN SCHOOL WOULD BE GREAT, AND
YOU WOULDN'T BE ALONE EITHER!

Oh, my dear, when I was a kid I went to school
and I missed my parents, too.
I have to work while you are at school,
but I will count the minutes until I see you.

Either by car, bus, train, or rocket,
I will come back to you.

And at the the end of the school day,
I will be waiting for you.

Reader's Note

For many kids, the start of preschool is the first time they are separated from their attachment figures—that is, the people who took care of them for the first few years of their life (parents, grandparents, nannies, etc.). Even the kids who have gone to daycare have some difficulty transitioning to preschool.

The start of preschool almost always involves a phase of crisis. Some children break down on the first day and refuse to let their attachment figures leave. Others run off to explore, immediately at ease, and say goodbye to attachment figures as if they're dismissing them. Then, weeks later, they refuse to go, seemingly out of nowhere. It's as if they are done exploring, have tried everything new, and now they want to return to their previous, familiar life. You know your child well, so try to follow their lead. Here are some things to keep in mind to ease their transition to school:

Stay Calm. To help a child learn to feel safe even in the absence of their attachment figure, the parent or caregiver will need to be (or at least appear!) calm at the moment of separation. Their faces send messages that help children interpret the situation and how to feel about it. Children take their cues from us; if we are upset, they are much more likely to be upset. If we are calm, there's a greater chance they will calm down. Don't, however, compare your child to other children ("see how brave he is?"). This is likely to just make them feel inadequate.

Create Excitement. Starting preschool is an important growth event for your child; try to convey this idea to them as well! *You are ready to go to school! You will meet new friends, learn new games, and explore a bigger world that's full of great things.* When they come home, ask about their day and what they learned, and listen attentively. If you are excited and interested, it's more likely they will be as well!

Try a Gradual Transition. When a child begins preschool, they need to remember a lot of new information: where to hang up their coat, what to do if they need to use the bathroom, who to tell if they don't feel well, etc. And they find themselves surrounded by lots of unfamiliar kids, who are just as disoriented as they are. A gradual transition may help with this information overload. Collaborate with your school and your teachers to figure out the best path to support your child.

Reinforce Their Autonomy. The primary objective of preschool is to help children feel that they are capable of doing things on their own. In this process, the role of parents and caregivers is very important: they need to be able to understand the child's basic need for autonomy and avoid trivializing or, worse, ignoring it. For example, let them walk to class rather than having you carry them. You can also let them try dressing and undressing themselves. When the child returns home, it's important to show interest and appreciation for what they did that day, and to listen attentively to their thoughts and the skills that they are developing.

ALBERTO PELLAI, MD, PhD, is a child psychotherapist and a researcher at the Department of Bio-medical Sciences of the University of Milan. In 2004 the Ministry of Health awarded him the silver medal of merit for public health. He is the author of numerous books for parents, teachers, teenagers, and children.
He lives in Italy.
Visit albertopellailibri.it
@alberto_pellai

BARBARA TAMBORINI is a psycho-pedagogist and writer. She leads workshops in schools for teachers and parents. She is the author with Alberto Pellai of several books aimed at parents. She lives in Somma, Italy.
@Barbara Tamborini

ELISA PAGANELLI is an award-winning illustrator and freelance designer.
She attended the Institute of Art and subsequently graduated in illustration from the European Institute of Design (IED) in Turin. Since, she has worked on over a hundred children's books. Elisa lives in the UK.
Visit elisapaganelli.com
@ElisaPaganelliillustrator
@elisaupsidedown
@elisapaganelli_illustration

MAGINATION PRESS is the children's book imprint of the American Psychological Association. Through APA's publications, the association shares with the world mental health expertise and psychological knowledge. Magination Press books reach young readers and their parents and caregivers to make navigating life's challenges a little easier. It's the combined power of psychology and literature that makes a Magination Press book special.
Visit www.maginationpress.org
@maginationpress

Books for Kids From the
American Psychological Association

Original Title: Non Voglio Andare a Scuola!
World copyright © 2018 DeA Planeta Libri S.r.l.

Magination Press is a registered trademark of the American Psychological Association. Order books at maginationpress.org, or call 1-800-374-2721.

English translation by Katie ten Hagen
Book design by Rachel Ross
Printed by Worzalla, Stevens Point, WI

Cataloging-in-Publication is on file at the Library of Congress.
ISBN-13: 978-1-4338-3244-4
LCCN: 2019055234

Manufactured in the United States of America
10 9 8 7 6 5 4 3 2 1